THE NEST

BEN ERRINGTON   DANIEL WILLCOCKS

ANDY CONDUIT-TURNER   JOHN CRINAN

OTHER TITLES BY HAWK & CLEAVER

Novels

Lazarus: Enter the Deadspace

They Rot (Book 1)

They Remain (Book 2)

Deeper than the Grave

The Hipster from Outer Space (Book 1)

The Hipster Who Leapt Through Time (Book 2)

Ten Tales of the Human Condition

Short Stories & Novellas

The Mark of the Damned

Twisted: A Collection of Dark Tales

Take the Corvus: Short Stories & Essays

Dye Pack / Oil Slick / Gut Spill

Death Throes & Other Short Stories

The Jump Series

Sins of Smoke

Breeder

Keep up-to-date at

www.hawkandcleaver.com

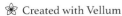 Created with Vellum

FOR

Every listener, reader, narrator, and creator, who has contributed to The Other Stories podcast.

5 million downloads, and counting.

A SPECIAL THANKS TO OUR PATRONS

Our patreon patrons are the lifeblood of Hawk & Cleaver. Without their constant support, we wouldn't be able to do what we do. Thanks a million for your constant support, no matter what level you fall into.

Raptors

Kathy Robinson . B. Lisa Kyer .
Scott Burgher . David Tolbert . Karm Parker

Hawks

Alisha Worth . Deborah Fagg . Ian McEuen . John Connelly . Josh Curran .
Karen Cooper . Larna Dennis . Luis Ochoa . Nancy Folsom . Nathan Abimelec . Nicole Daenzer . Nicole Parks . Paul Collins . Ryan Lockhart

Hatchlings

Want your name featured in all future Hawk & Cleaver books? Visit www.patreon.com/hawkandcleaver to find out how.

FOREWORD

The tale you are about to embark on is bigger than anything we've ever done before.

Not story-wise, in particular. Hawk & Cleaver have produced a handful of novels and works which extend far beyond the word count in this novella. I'm talking about the podcast, and the world behind this story.

The Other Stories is an untamed beast. By the time this book hits publication in two days, the podcast will have already accumulated an additional 20,000 downloads. We began the show with one. One download, from one listener who trusted us enough to spend some time getting lost in our fictional worlds. One listener who created the snowball effect and got this monster running downhill. It's far too big and heavy now to stop. A colossal cyclops sprinting down a track, accumulating debris along its way and turning into some titanic thing that has a life of its own.

That's a hell of an analogy, but it's true.

The more time goes by, the more it feels as though

we've found our tribe. We were four creators looking to make something bigger than ourselves. We were fans of horror. Fans of the short story medium. And, by some serendipitous force, we found an entire world of listeners who share our passion, writers who contribute and live in the world of horror, and narrators who bring it all to life.

Let's also not forget an audio producer with ears more tuned into the microscopic detail than a goddamn bat.

The Other Stories is big, now, and Halloween has always been where we have reached the most listeners. Even those who don't usually indulge in horror find the time to give themselves some spooks. In 2018 we were lucky enough to bring Bram Stoker Award-Winner, Kealan Patrick Burke, into our little community and share one of his incredible tales, and in this year (2019), we're bringing the podcast its first ever 5-part serial.

That's this book (in case you haven't guessed). The Nest combines the talents of four regular contributors to the podcast, and each one of them has been instrumental to its success. I'm not going to be self-indulgent here and talk about myself, but what I will do is say a massive thank you to Ben Errington, Andy Conduit-Turner, and John Crinan for all of their contributions in making this story happen. Collaboration can always be a tough nut to crack, but what has come out of the brains of four horror freaks is something that we're all very proud of. This adventure was a lot of fun, and as much as we like to spook, I hope the fun comes through.

Special mention here also goes to Luke Kondor, our show wrangler and producer. Extra special thanks to our captain of audio, and production wizard, Karl Hughes (who has been monumental in making this happen), as well as each and every narrator who has contributed to the audio version of this tale: Alexandra Elroy, Josh Curran, Persephone Rose, and Jasmine Arch. Despite all of the trials of bringing this story alive, we got there. It's done. You guys rock!

The Other Stories may be our greatest creation to date. With over 40 themes, each featuring four 20-minute episodes, and a whole host of Patreon-exclusive content, we've produced over 50 hours of free horror content for listeners across the world. By picking up this book, you are becoming a part of that journey, and bringing this story to a brand-new medium. That's pretty cool, don't you think?

The tale you are about to embark on is bigger than anything we've ever done before. From all of us here at Hawk & Cleaver, we hope you have as much fun reading this as we did making it together.

Until next time,

Daniel Willcocks
26th October, 2019

THE NEST

1

JAMIE

Jamie stood at the edge of the mall forecourt and watched the steady stream of passers-by, examining them from behind his sunglasses to ensure he was not recognized. It would be a total disaster if one of his classmate's parents saw him skulking around a shopping establishment a solid two hours before school was due to finish for the day.

When he was convinced that the coast was clear, he made his way into the mall and took the stairs to the second floor, avoiding the elevators where the bloated and wheezing security guard seemed to spend half of his shift. He knew that he'd have no problem outrunning him if he needed to, the man was well into his fifties, but he'd prefer to remain unseen during this particular shoplifting excursion.

He approached the RadioShack electronics store, aware that his window of opportunity would be small before the cashier—a bearded and bespectacled man in his thirties—would start to suspect him. Luckily, the store was fairly busy, and Jamie knew exactly what he needed and where in the store to find it.

He would prefer to not have to steal, of course, however Jamie felt that theft was his only option. His mother gave him a regular allowance, which he was grateful for, but it was meagre and didn't cover even a small percentage of his daily necessities.

Jamie spent most of this money on cigarettes, which he was certainly addicted to by now, the fine sprouting of short ginger hairs on his chin making him pass for the minimum age of sixteen that was required to buy them. He'd read in a newspaper that this limit was soon going to be increased to eighteen, which he was sure would impact his nicotine consumption greatly.

He enjoyed Camel Lights, which according to the packaging had 'Low Tar & Camel Taste'. Jamie wasn't entirely sure what camels tasted like, but he doubted it was similar to inhaling bitter cigarette smoke.

He knew some older boys who were closer to that age, but the thought of asking somebody else to aid his smoking habit made him feel silly. Perhaps he would give up, but not right away. He'd do it closer to Christmas so he would have more spare money to add to the 'Nintendo Fund' he had started with his younger brother, Frank. It currently stood at $12, nowhere near enough to buy a brand-new NES let alone the accompanying games. That was something he definitely couldn't steal due to the fact that video game consoles were usually kept under lock and key out of reach behind counters rather than on the shop floor.

Jamie needed a 2-way radio as his last model had met the undignified end of being trampled on by his mother during one of her regular late-night wine binges. She had stumbled into his room, waking him up to kiss him goodnight and slur '*I love you sweetie*' into his ear while slobbering all over his cheek, crashing around on her way out and smashing his TRC-214 Walkie Talkie to bits. He heard the plastic casing crack, watching with annoyance as his mother trudged out, her fluffy slippers barely noticing the damage they had done.

Jamie was good with tech and knew plenty about 2-way radios, so much so that he could improve them beyond the state they arrived directly from the manufacturer. He could improve their range and durability, but the TRC was beyond fixing after its run-in with his inebriated mother.

Jamie kept his head down as he entered the store, a cool blast of air conditioning sending a shiver down his neck and blowing his red hair across his forehead.

RadioShack was one of only three places in the mall with a CCTV camera installed and it just so happened to be pointed on an angle that Jamie could avoid once he got to the end of the aisle that was stocked with most of the radios. The TRC-214 was in this blind spot, away from the high-end and expensive equipment that Jamie would have to work 25 summers mowing lawns to be able to afford.

Jamie scanned the shelves for the product that he required, a three-watt three-channel CB radio stored in a blue and white striped box. There was just the one in stock, the end of the box split open and a corner of the clear polythene that protected the Walkie Talkie inside was spilling out. Jamie knew that he wouldn't be asking the cashier if there was one in better condition in the storeroom, so with a quick look over his shoulder and then another down the adjacent aisle, he swung his bright yellow backpack from his shoulder to the ground, unzipped it and bundled the radio inside in one swift motion.

Jamie was back on his feet, his Nike basketball shoes (also stolen) squeaking on the floor as he marched back the way he had come in. He left RadioShack, his backpack considerably heavier than before, and turned back to the store to see the cashier showing an Asian woman a pair of extravagant looking headphones through the glass.

He clenched his fists in triumph. He had made it.

As he rounded a corner, he collided hard with the mall security guard, bouncing against the man's rotund stomach and nearly falling backwards. Jamie gasped and leaned onto his heels, ready to make a run for it.

"Hey!" the security guard yelped, like a dog that had its tail trodden on. "Watch it, kid!"

Jamie walked around him without a word and began descending the stairs to the ground floor.

"Shouldn't you be in school?" the security guard called after him, neon lights from the nearby arcade reflecting off of his balding, sweat-speckled head.

"I guess so," Jamie shrugged.

It was too quiet for the security guard to hear. Plus, he didn't seem to care. He turned away and continued coughing into a handkerchief that made Jamie feel queasy as he imagined the fabric filling with the man's slimy mucus.

The kid had a sudden realisation that he'd be doing

the same in years to come unless he kicked the Camel habit.

JAMIE MADE SURE THAT HE TIMED HIS ARRIVAL AT HOME perfectly so that it seemed to his mother that he had spent the day at school and finished at the appropriate time.

The bus took almost 45 minutes to get from the mall and up into the hills of Creekwood Pines, the small town where he had lived his entire life. It took even longer to get there from the school, so his truancy and diversion were taken into account when he approached the front door of number four Hewson Drive. The street was a cul-de-sac in an ordinary suburban area where the houses looked the same and were mostly populated by families although everyone kept to themselves. When the sky was dark and brooding, he felt like he lived in a graveyard.

His mother had been drinking again last night, singing along to Elvis Presley records until the early hours of the morning, meaning that she wouldn't have made it out of bed until at least midday. Even then, she'd have been nursing a hangover from the couch, and although it was unlikely that somebody would call the house to check on Jamie's whereabouts, he had the presence of mind to remember to unplug the phone before he had left that morning and he could guarantee that she wouldn't notice it wasn't working.

Nobody called them. Not unless a bill was overdue, or it was even worse news.

It was raining lightly, the clouds that had congregated in the sky refusing to commit to a downpour. As Jamie opened the front door he needed to kick and lift the expanding wood as he unlocked it. It needed repairing, but much like many of the problems with the house, it was likely to be ignored by his mother until it became a serious problem.

The first thing Jamie noticed was that the house was freezing cold. His mother would usually crank electric heaters up to their highest setting at this time of year, no matter how much Jamie and Frank complained. The boys would often find themselves wearing shorts around the house as if they were on the beach.

"Mom?" Jamie called out as he pushed the door closed with a thud.

If she didn't immediately respond it would mean that she was asleep somewhere, probably on the couch with an empty wine glass in hand and some trash show on TV. But Jamie couldn't hear a soap opera or a game show at the usual unbearable volume. He couldn't hear a thing.

"*Mom*?" Jamie repeated as he stepped from the hall into the living room, his voice shrill.

It was empty, a pile of blankets on the couch and a full glass of orange juice on the coffee table. The ashtray next to it was overflowing with long stubbed out cigarette butts. The television was off, but it had been pushed outward and was facing towards the kitchen. As he moved into the centre of the room, he noticed a chair on its side and an upturned plate next to the dining table.

There was food, some remnants of macaroni cheese, smushed into the carpet.

The curtains were drawn, and the only source of light was a flickering lamp in the corner. The room was gloomy and for a brief, fleeting secondJamie felt afraid. The kind of fear that would chase after you when you turned off the lights downstairs and ran up to your bedroom, half-expecting a skinned demon to be clawing at your heels.

Jamie walked to the corner of the room and leaned over the armchair where nobody ever sat, checking that the phone remained unplugged. Once he saw that it was, he fished around in the darkness for the cord and pushed it back into the wall.

The phone sat on a mahogany side-table where more cigarette butts were scattered, the receiver not quite in its cradle. He nudged it back in place and went to the kitchen.

His mother wasn't there either and the fridge was wide open. He closed it, taking a mental note of all of the oddities that added to her bewildering absence. He couldn't recall a single time that she hadn't been at home when he returned from school.

He felt his throat constrict with anxiety as he made his way upstairs and checked the rooms up there. Her bedroom was empty, and the bed was perfectly made, almost as if it hadn't been slept in at all. Frank's room was empty too, a mess of superhero and wrestler action figures piled into the middle of the room. Jamie's room was far more presentable, but when he stood on the fraying rug, his mind running wild with speculative thoughts of his mother hanging from her neck by a rope, he noticed a hairline crack in the glass of the window.

He moved closer, the sky that backlit the tiny break now blackening as a storm threatened, holding out one hand to touch the window. He ran his finger back and forth over the crack and as he looked down into the yard and saw something strange.

Puzzled, Jamie made his way downstairs and back into the living room where he knocked over the glass of orange juice from the coffee table onto the carpet with a clunk and a splash as he absentmindedly ambled towards the kitchen. There, he fumbled with the dead-bolt of the backdoor, opening it wide to be greeted by a sturdy rush of wind.

He scampered into the garden, tripping over raised patio slabs as he got closer to what looked like a scattering of large dark feathers, as if a huge bird had been attacked by something impossibly bigger. He'd seen it before, the carnage left behind after a bird had been pounced on and torn into by the talons of an owl, but these feathers didn't look like they could belong to owl prey.

Jamie sat on the couch inside the house, his backpack still on as he tried to call the one person who might know where his mother was, a woman with red cheeks and wire wool hair named Shelley who sometimes gossiped with her on Sunday afternoons whilst drinking home-made mojitos in the yard. He found her number in a leather-bound phone book, but when he called it just rang out.

He thought about calling his Uncle John, but he knew

that he'd probably just tell him to stop being a pussy and not to worry.

Jamie was frustrated and had convinced himself that he was overreacting by the time the front door bumped open. He felt a brief swell of relief which was instantly doused when he realized it was just Frank coming back from soccer practice.

"I'm *starving*!" he yelled.

Jamie appeared next to him as he closed the door.

"Mom's not here," he said with concern.

Frank looked unbothered.

"Maybe she went for groceries," he suggested, throwing his muddied boots onto the ground.

"*Really*?" Jamie said, "When was the last time she went for groceries? I've got all the food stamps in a drawer in my room."

Frank shrugged and started padding upstairs towards his bedroom where Jamie knew he intended to spend the rest of his evening acting out fantasy wrestling matches between Spider-Man and Hulk Hogan.

"Frank?" Jamie called after him. "This is *weird*."

The kid didn't respond.

Jamie listened to Frank's footsteps as he walked into his room and heard a thump as he dropped his sports bag.

"If she's not here," Frank shouted, as if he'd been suddenly presented with a revelation, "Then I'm having ice cream for dinner!"

Several hours went by and as it grew dark outside, Jamie had been swept up in the newfound freedom having no adult in the house meant for him and Frank, despite the fact that his mother had never been particularly strict.

Halloween was approaching, and although that was the last thought on Jamie's mind, it was clearly a priority for Frank.

The brothers gathered in the living room in front of the television, a VHS of '*Night of the Living Dead*'(a movie that their mother would never have let Frank know existed let alone watch) playing whilst the younger of the two put the final touches to his '*Teen Wolf*' costume that he'd impressively hand-made.

A half-full bowl of mostly melted mint chocolate-chip ice cream was at his feet and he was paying no attention to the groaning zombies on the screen.

Jamie was lying on the couch, staring at his toe poking through a hole in his sock.

"You should eat something, Frank," Jamie said.

Frank was cutting some red fabric with scissors.

"I am eating something," he said, nodding to the bowl.

"I mean something that *isn't* dessert," Jamie added. "I can cook something for you. How about a grilled cheese?"

Frank didn't answer. He was biting his lip as he concentrated on loosely measuring a strip of the fabric.

Jamie sat up with a start. All of a sudden, he remembered that his friend Raheem had been off sick from school all week, a nasty cold leaving him stuck in his bedroom whilst his Dad worked one of his three jobs.

Raheem was a weird kid, but Jamie thought he was

cool. He had a telescope and a pair of binoculars, often acting like a member of the neighborhood watch as he monitored those who lived nearby, convinced that the residents were lizards in human suits or members of satanic cults.

If anybody had witnessed something suspicious or even seen his mother leave the house, it would be Raheem. Plus, he had a two-way radio.

Jamie took his backpack into his bedroom and switched on the table lamp on a wooden sideboard that was the hub of his 'workshop', various tools strewn across it and scrawled notes on scraps of paper. He took out the TRC-214 box and opened it up, removed all of the packaging, fixed a fresh battery inside and began to tune into Raheem's frequency.

Something is wrong, he immediately thought as the radio picked up static and a few whirs and whistles at the other end. The rain was coming down hard outside now, a heavy torrent of water pounding hard against the window.

He realized what the problem could be. He stood up and walked to the window, opening it wide as the howling storm tried to take it from its hinges and Jamie's head along with it.

He looked out and up, noticing that the antenna he had mounted on his roof to boost the Walkie Talkie signal had come loose, the rain and wind tearing it down. It clung on for dear life but Jamie knew he had to reposition it before it fell towards the yard, no doubt ending up bent out of shape and unusable after dropping onto the patio.

He ran downstairs to put his sneakers back on and

realized that Frank was now staring directly at the TV as a zombie child stabbed a woman to death with a trowel, unflinching at the gore.

Back upstairs, Jamie climbed onto the window ledge with the radio in his hand, reaching desperately towards the guttering. He edged along, the wind swooping up his varsity jacket like a cape.

He held on tight to the side of the house and felt around blindly for the antenna, taking hold of it and haphazardly fixing it back into place. It wouldn't last, but as long as he could talk to Raheem, even for a few minutes, it would suffice.

The ice-cold rain struck his face as the radio squealed, Raheem's urgent broken voice erupting from the speaker.

"JamJaCome in!"

Jamie's right foot slipped, and he almost plummeted towards the ground.

"Jamie! Can you he?"

A split sharp edge of the guttering had latched onto Jamie's sleeve and his hair was in his eyes as he struggled to find his way back into the window.

"JaA flyingDon't goDon't go outsi!"

Jamie awkwardly tore himself free with the hand that was holding the radio, managing to turn around so that his back was to the window.

"Jamie! There's a flying! Did you get th? A flying!"

A dark shape shrieked as it came up from the yard and into the sky, its otherworldly size blending into the darkness as it moved. Wings flapped hard, the width of whatever it was causing Jamie to scream as he fell backwards into the open window, landing hard on the carpeted floor, his shoulder taking the brunt of the impact. The radio slipped from his grasp and rolled under his bed as the shadow moved over the house, a venomous screech following closely.

Jamie sat up, wiping the rainwater from his face, his breathing rapid and his heart feeling like an inflating balloon in his chest.

He was unsure what he had seen or if it had really been as enormous as it seemed. That shriek... it was unlike anything he had heard before. It sounded like fingernails on a chalkboard and glass shattering and car gears grinding all at once.

"Jamie!"

Frank was calling from downstairs. He sounded terrified. Panicked, Jamie leapt up from the floor and almost fell down the stairs as he took them three at a time, running to the aid of his sibling.

In the living room, zombies were eating a man on the TV and Frank wasn't watching anymore. His '*Teen Wolf*' costume was in a heap on the floor.

"*Jamie!*"

He called again from the kitchen. As Jamie reached him, Frank was kneeling down with the back door open, the storm bizarrely and promptly subsiding. There was a distant silent flash of lightning.

"There was something clawing at the door," Frank said, calmly. "It sounded like a dog. A *big* dog."

Frank had retrieved a flashlight from a kitchen cupboard and was aiming a beam of white light at something on the step just outside of the door. Jamie knelt down beside him.

There was a package that looked like it was made up

of shredded clothes and padded with dirt, spilling out worms and cockroaches from the top like an under-cooked insect pie. It was moving, as if the creatures had been packed in tight and were escaping from every crack and crevice, wriggling for freedom.

On top of the parcel was a pair of spectacles, the frames splintered and drops of rainwater pouring from them like tears. Jamie recognized them right away.

They belonged to his mother.

2

VALERIE

Valerie Townsend had been prepared for a night of sleepless rest, but it hadn't exactly gone as planned.

Her birthday was tomorrow. The big one-six. One of the oldest in her year, she felt a slight discomfort at reaching yet another aging milestone. She was already the butt of so many jokes from her friends about how creepy it was that she hung out with the younger kids, but the truth was far from that.

Her mom had famously babysat half the neighborhood's kids, meaning that, with her father busy keeping peace in the sleepy lumber town, Valerie often had to accompany her. A by-product of which meant she made friends with some of the kids in the lower grades.

So what?

It wasn't even like she had fun doing it. For several uneasy years she had actually acted as the surrogate mom of the houses, changing diapers, mopping drool, and fixing cheap broken toys while her own mother sat downstairs watching crappy reruns of *The Price is Right*, switching between gossiping on the phone with her gal pals and snoozing on the sofa.

When the kids' parents returned home, her mother had a strangely impressive habit of being able to switch to 'Supermom' and grasp for Valerie's hard-earned cash like a crack-addict scratching for a fix.

Which would still have been a sore subject of conversation, were her mom still in her life.

But none of that was the reason that Valerie couldn't sleep that night. No, surely, she should have been giddy with excitement at what the wonder of her birthday would bring. Surely she should be buzzing with joy at the prospect of cake and balloons, of seeing friends and receiving presents, of being showered in kisses and hugs from loved ones.

Yet, the real reason that she couldn't sleep, had been the howling of the wind outside.

The weathermen had predicted it a few days ago. A small storm blowing into the side of the town. The man with creases in his brow and a caterpillar moustache who crackled on the old 8-inch TV said it wouldn't be anything to worry about. Perhaps some branches would break, perhaps some power lines might go down. "But it will be in and out in a jiffy," he chuckled, waving a hand across the map behind him while her father scoffed at the innuendo.

And at first there had been some truth in his words. On her way to school that day the wind had picked up. Trash blew across the ground and clattered towards the roads. Leaves flew like colored pencil shavings, all the hues of the fall season. High school children braced their coats and clung tightly to their bags as wind whipped at their hair and blew fine particles of dust their way, irritating eyes and making throats dry.

But then, as the sun faded and the moon had risen high in the cloud-spotted sky, the winds had gone berserk.

It came out of nowhere. One minute, wind hushed through the small cracks around her windowsill, whispering like conspiratorial lovers. The next the glass had rattled in the cases and the trees had bent beyond anything she had seen. It was as though a tornado had threatened to appear, then vanished as quickly as it had come. Fluttering away and deflating like a burst party balloon.

Yet, even with all that, that wasn't the real reason she couldn't sleep that night.

The real reason had been the chuckling shrieks that called over the top of the wind. The shrill, howling cackle of a witch with a bad throat, followed by the strange shape that had flown past her window. Large and passerine. Laced with feathers and an impressive wingspan.

Combine that with the several hours of horror movies she'd watched without her father's knowledge before bed, and—there you have it—the perfect concoction to induce insomnia in a pubescent high school girl. A Halloween treat designed to keep even the boldest of warriors awake until the early dawn.

"Morning pumpkin," Valerie's dad said absently as he ruffled his newspaper and waited for his toast to pop. He was already alert and dressed, looking sharp in his Sheriff's uniform. One of the few full-time law enforcement operatives in Creekwood Pines, Valerie was almost certain that his head was already full of leads and investigations which would occupy the majority of his day. It was the same most of the time. She'd gotten used to her father never fully being present in the house, particularly since her mother had left. "Sleep okay?"

Valerie rubbed her tired eyes. They looked bruised, dark hammocks hung underneath. She walked over to the cupboards and grabbed a box of Dinky Donuts cereal. She began pouring them into a bowl.

"Hmmm."

"Hell of a wind last night. Did you hear it? Damn near shook the house down. You just know I'm going to have a thousand messages asking me to check out shed doors which have opened and windows which have blown out their frames." He looked up briefly from his paper. "What am I meant to do about it? It's not like it was a robbery. Just old lady Renee and her WI group thinking that a burglar had attacked them because they sleep so deeply, they may as well be practicing for death."

Valerie shrugged.

"Strangest thing, though. A gust like that. I mean, I've never seen anything like it. Came and went like that," he snapped his fingers. "That was impressive, even by this town's standards."

Valerie sat at the table and ate her breakfast. Tiredness stole the sugary taste from the cereal and before she knew it, she had her backpack shouldered and was heading out of the door.

Her father was gone before she'd gone downstairs. All

final hopes of him remembering her special day long gone out of the window. Years back had been different. Whole mornings off school to unwrap presents and eat pancakes in the living room. But now...

Francis, Valerie's tabby cat, appeared from the other room and trotted over to her feet. She stalked figure eights between her legs and purred.

"At least you didn't forget, eh, buddy?" she said, bending to give Francis a quick stroke before heading out the door.

There was still a fair kick to the wind. Nothing by the gust's standards, but the weatherman had certainly predicted true. Had Valerie been one of the girls who spent hours before school making their hair perfect and padding their faces with make-up, she may have been pissed off at this point. Her hair flew around her as if it had a life of its own. She held one strap of her backpack and bunched clumps of hair in her other fist just in order to see the traffic and cross the road.

Some birthday, she thought as she saw Lesley Robbins standing by the school gates. She caught her eye and waved her down, jogging to catch up.

"Happy birthday," Lesley smirked, pulling a hastily wrapped package, wrapped tightly in Sellotape, from her pocket.

"Thanks," Valerie replied. "I was starting to wonder if I'd gotten the wrong date, myself."

"What are you talking about?"

Valerie looked out from under the shelf of her eyebrows.

"Oh, right. He didn't forget again, did he?"

A bell rang, calling the first class of the day. Valerie

and Lesley began walking. "Of course, he did. I don't know why I expect anything less. Since him and mom broke up, all he cares about is his stupid job. I can see why she left him in the first place."

"I thought *he* left *her*?"

"Po-tay-to, po-tah-to," Valerie held up the package to the light, as if trying to see through the paper. "The end result is all the same, isn't it? They're no longer together, and I'm stuck in this shitty backwards town miles from anywhere with a father who spends more time with strangers than he does his own daughter. Honestly, sometimes I wish I could just... Y'know... Run away and go live on my own."

"You wouldn't last two seconds out there," Lesley scoffed. "Besides, who knows, maybe he's planning a big *surprise* party after you get home? What better way to surprise you than pretend to forget it's your birthday?" They rounded a corridor and joined the line queueing for their first class of the day. Home Ec. Great.

Valerie ignored the latter part of Lesley's comments. "I'd last a whole sight longer than you. Just because your Dad is a friggin' mechanic and mine is hardly home, doesn't mean I don't know how to handle myself."

"Puh-lease," Lesley laughed. "You can't even open that present by yourself. How would you handle yourself in the big wide world?"

Valerie, who had been trying to find a small section of the package to tear open, shoved the package in her pocket. "I'm not even trying. And what's that got to do with anything?" She brushed her hair out of her face, aware of how hot her cheeks had grown. "Forget it, happy birthday to me, now let's get this shitty day over with."

To her great relief, classes went fast that day. It wasn't even a bad line up of classes after Home Ec. Valerie actually found she liked school—considerably more since her best friend was in a lot of the same classes as her—and soon they had passed through maths, English, and chemistry.

When the bell sounded for lunch, the class abruptly climbed up from their desks and filed out the door. Dozens upon dozens of students choked the corridors, eagerly revelling in the opportunity to catch up with friends and ram some food down their throats.

There was a whole buzz of excitement at the storm currently building outside. Valerie caught snippets of people's conversations as she squeezed through the halls, little realising before how many students there were, since most lunchtimes everyone was outside on the playground or out on the sports field to stretch their legs, gossip, and hurl balls around.

"I jumped out of my skin!" Tammy Horton, a ninth grader with braces and a reputation for exaggeration, regaled to Gina Treskall and Harley Dickson. "Dad came in and thought a burglar had come into my room because of how loudly the tree whacked my window. When he realized it was just the wind, he just started laughing."

"Did he not hear that screech?" Gina asked. "I heard it. I thought maybe a car was skidding down our road, but then I swore I saw something out there."

"Saw something? Like what?" Harley laughed. More immune to Tammy's stories than the rest, her face was placid and bored. She blew out a mouthful of air. "What? Are you going to tell me that some creature was out there in the wind last night? I saw a telephone pole nearly blow over. You think *anything* would have survived in that weather? They'd be halfway out onto Route 19 by now."

Tammy caught Valerie's eye, then looked away. Lesley pulled Valerie's hand to keep her moving through the corridor.

There were dozens of mentions of the event from last night. Several more of something dark and strange taking to the skies. Some speculated a vampire (yeah, right!), some said it was probably the top of a gazebo caught in the gust, there were even a few suggestions that there was nothing at all, and that the whole thing had been nothing more than a shared dream. A phenomenon that happens only occasionally but can be caused by shared distress in certain weather conditions.

"Whatever it was, I just hope it doesn't happen again," Lesley said after pulling Valerie away and out of sight from Isabel, a girl in the younger years who had often pushed the boundaries of what the school considered to be 'suitable uniform,' and who had taken a liking to shooting her sharp tongue at Valerie in the halls. They eventually found a quieter area towards the back of the school, beneath the cubby where the stairs to the upper levels folded back on themselves.

Valerie chewed her lip, hoping the same thing. All through her classes she had fought off sleep, enduring nightmare flashes of scenes she'd seen in her movies last night, and all-the-while her mind fought off that horrendous screech that had come. Something otherworldly through the spirit of her unconsciousness and into a waking reality...

Excited voices. A group of eighth graders appeared

down the stairs, heads tucked closely together as they discussed animatedly.

"Hey! What are you guys jabbering about?" Valerie called, jumping out from under the stairs.

The four boys near enough jumped out of their skin. Their faces fell from fear, to relief, to laughter when they saw Valerie.

She knew the boys. *Had* known them well, at one point. Only, the last time she had truly spent any real time with them was years back, babysitting Harold and Jonathon's little siblings with her mother. Enduring their slumber parties and evening hangouts while scooping popcorn from a bowl and ensuring her mother didn't choke on her own tongue as she snoozed.

"You shouldn't jump out at us like that," Harold blurted, poking his tongue out.

"We'll tell Miss Rixton you're bullying us," Jonathon chided.

Liam rolled his eyes. "No you won't, you're scared shit-less of Miss Rixton. You cower every time you pass her door."

"Oi, language!" Valerie said, her parental instinct kicking into gear. She caught herself, and blushed, remembering that, while they were still several years younger than her, they weren't toddlers anymore. She noticed something amiss about the group. "Hey, where's the other one?"

Harold looked shiftily at the floor. "What other one?"

"You know what other one. Jamie. Shouldn't he be with you guys? I thought you lot were inseparable?"

"Don't know!" George Hallam, the weediest of the group, shrugged. "He's not in."

"Haven't seen him all morning. Probably bunking off," Jonathan added.

"Yeah, right," Harold chided. "Like Jamie's mom would let him bunk off. Come on. Let's go."

Valerie eyed the group curiously as they left. She had met Jamie's mother. Had smelt her whiskey breath and seen her harsh hand. She certainly would never have allowed Jamie to run truant. She eyed them curiously as a sudden flash of the dark creature from the night sky flashed into her mind.

What the hell is going on with this damn storm?

THINGS GOT A WHOLE LOT WEIRDER THE MOMENT VALERIE stepped through the door.

She hadn't expected her father to be home. Not really. Although she'd be lying if she said that Lesley's words hadn't gotten under her skin. As she turned the handle and let herself into her house, she closed her eyes and held her breath, the smallest part of her—the part that still believed that somewhere in the world magic existed—waited for the sudden outburst of family and friends as the surprise party kicked into full gear.

What met her eyes, though, was something else entirely.

"What the"

The house had been ransacked. Side tables were upturned, vases smashed on the floor, the muddy contents of her father's ficus trodden into the carpet. She dropped her bag. Her hand found her mouth. Pictures were knocked askew and there was something that looked like blood on the floor.

And that was just the hallway.

The kitchen and the living room weren't much different. Something had happened here. All the tell-tale signs of a struggle hit her like a physical force. Her heart quickened. Her breath caught. She ran from room to room, not entirely sure what she was meant to do in this situation.

She circled back to the blood, a sudden possibility echoing around her head.

"Dad…"

He hadn't been due home. Shouldn't have been back from the office until later. Usually at this time he'd be down at the Sheriff's office or out dealing with a call. Valerie would prepare something half-assed and wholesome so that he could keep his strength up when he returned home later, then they'd watch shitty TV until 9pm when Dad would give a half-hearted attempt at enforcing a bedtime and Valerie would disappear to her room to watch movies.

Then whose blood was that?

Valerie found herself at the house phone. A bulky orange thing connected to the wall by a long, coiled wire.

"Hello, Sam?" Sammy was her father's assistant. A desk-jockey who handled phone calls and paperwork to free up her dad's time. "Sam, is that you?"

"Valerie?" Sammy chuckled. A sickly-sweet bag of delights to all she spoke to. "Hello, how are you dear? Are you okay? You sound flustered."

"Can I speak to my dad please? Is he there?"

Sammy considered this. In the moment's pause of quiet, Valerie felt time stretch like taffy between parting hands. "Why, no. He's been across town investigating some disturbances. In fact, oh, actually, he asked me not to say…"

"What? Not say what?" Valerie could feel herself panicking now.

"Well… Okay. Consider this your birthday present from mebut don't tell your father, okay?"

Valerie promised she wouldn't.

"There have been calls from across town of some disturbances. A little boy rang and said that his mother was even missing. A call came from the house across from yours. Elton Sheeply across the street phoned it in. Said he could see someone there. Your dad went to investigate and he"

"The boy. Was his name Jamie?" Valerie asked without hesitation.

"How did you" Sammy gasped. "Wait a second. You're not at your house *now* are you?"

But Sammy was talking into an empty receiver. The phone hung limply from the wall, ticking like a pendulum. Valerie had heard enough to start panicking.

Her father had been here.

Someone had been inside the house with him.

And now, taking steps that felt weighted with lead, she followed the trail of blood along the carpet. The small splashes ending in a larger splat against the chintzy wallpaper.

Valerie's breath caught. Sticking out from beneath the upturned side table was a rigid grey tail. She nudged the table aside and saw Francis' body, slashed and torn into ribbons.

Uttering a choked sob, Valerie shouldered her pack

and high-tailed it out of her house, a fleeting thought coming to her as she tore down Ashdale Street and turned onto Hewson Drive.

Dad remembered, after all. How else would Sammy have known?

≈

VALERIE'S FISTS BANGED URGENTLY AGAINST THE DOOR. It was still light out, but dusk was falling fast. Gold-dappled sunlight fell in thick rays across the street as several nosy neighbors peeked through their curtains to find out what was making all that noise.

"Come on, come come, come on," Valerie muttered beneath her breath. Then, "I know you're in there!"

A few seconds later and a head appeared around the door. A thirteen-year-old boy who looked as if his mom had just walked in on his first self-exploration into the realms of self-pleasure.

"Valerie? What are you"

Valerie shoved the door aside and let herself in. She slammed the door behind, hand running through her wild hair, eyes wide.

"Your mom is missing, isn't she?"

The color drained from the boy's face. "How did you..."

Valerie grabbed his shoulders, staring fiercely into his eyes. "Because my Dad is gone, too."

3

ISABEL

"I can't believe you'd do that to your beautiful hair!"

Variations of this phrase were all Isabel's mother had managed to utter since the grand reveal of her daughter's new look, when Isabel stepped into the kitchen for dinner. In an attempt to delay the inevitable argument that was brewing, Isabel didn't respond. Silently skewering another fork-full of Meatloaf from her plate she turned to watch the rain outside. The backyard was now far more like a swamp than a garden, the swing and rear fence at the edge of their property, completely obscured by the gloom and relentless sheets of water running down the glass. The weather had been getting steadily worse all week, so much so that school had been cancelled today. Aside from the bus drivers refusing to make the rounds in the growing storm, the old building's roof had so many leaks, that many of the classrooms were utterly unusable.

"It's still really coming down out there," Isabel sighed as she continued to stare out of the window, half expecting no reply as she began to wonder how she'd make it out tonight without ruining her hair.

Sadly for Isabel, her mother, who clearly had no intention of letting her daughter's choices go unchallenged; bulldozed straight through the vague attempt at small talk.

Slamming her palms on the table with a force that made each plate and piece of cutlery resting on it jolt and rattle she began the lecture she'd clearly been working herself up to for several minutes now.

"Don't change the subject young lady! Really, what do you expect me, or anyone for that matter to think? Forcing your hair to stand straight up like that is one thing, but dying it neon pink?! The whole town will be"

At this point Isabel took the bait and responded sharply.

"Will be what Mom? Beside themselves with panic that there's someone who doesn't have one of the three approved haircuts in the Shit-Heap town? Whispers of a girl in Creekwood Pines who's had an original thought?!"

Isabel gave a theatrical gasp, as she clapped her hands on either side of her face in an exaggerated expression of shock.

"Do you suppose they'll have a task-force drive all the way down here from Fleetwood to arrest me for disturbing the peace? Or will they just get together, community style, and burn me as a witch?"

"Cut the faux dramatics Isabella!"

Her mother didn't waste any time getting back on the offensive, and using her full name was a favorite tactic to show how serious she was. Isabel folded her arms and leaned back in her chair as she braced herself.

"Like it or not. We live in a small town. People know each other, and people talk. You've no idea what it's like! I had to quit the book club thanks to all the awkward looks and hushed gossip after that business between you and the Townsend girl the other month. Maybe you thrive on this type of negative attention and the horrified looks as you walk down the street, but I don't!"

"Mom, surely not everyone in town is"

"Enough of them are!" Her mother interrupted. Social things, I can let go, you've had a tough year, and I get it. But I have to see people in the shop every day."

"So, what you're saying is that you care more about what your customers think of *you* as a mother than you care about *me* being who I am?"

Isabel huffed. Tightening her crossed her arms she purposefully stared out of the window, denying her mother any form of eye contact to make her point.

Her expression softening a little, Isabel's mother slid her hand across the table towards her daughter. Isabel noted the olive branch being offered, and stubbornly ignored it, as her mother continued.

"Issy, when those people see that, hair and those clothes, they judge you. Not for who you are, but how those things make you look. They don't see an independent, creative young woman. They see a degenerate thug that picks fights with other girls at school that you should steer well clear of."

"Suits me just fine," Isabel snarled. "There's hardly anyone in this whole town worth talking to anyway."

"You don't mean that sweetheart," Isabel's mother had an almost pleading tone in her voice.

"I know you make out like you're this big bad loner

who doesn't need anybody, but I know you want friends and to just hang out like a normal teenager. It wasn't so different when I was growing up, you know?"

Looking at her mother with a smirk and a sideways glance, Isabel let her sullen demeanour slip a little.

"Come on now, Mom, I know this is a pretty wild look but it's hardly running halfway across the country in Grandpa's camper and returning it… *Stinking to high heaven of pot smokeso bad I had to sell the damned thing!*" Isabel even surprised herself at how passable an impression of her grandfather she'd been able to muster. "I've dyed my hair Mom, not taken up Freebasing or joined this generation's Manson Family."

Her mother flushed slightly and tried to stifle a smirk of her own. Isabel relaxed her arms, resting one on the table which allowed her mother's outstretched hand to meet hers.

"You think maybe we can look at the style, together before school reopens? Maybe we can find a way for you to express yourself, that won't get me summoned for a meeting with that dork, Principal Weil."

"Promise not to use the word dork again and I'll think about it."

Isabel's mother squeezed her arm with a smile before she began gathering up the dinner plates and clearing the table, leaving Isabel to finish the last few mouthfuls of her own meal.

"I guess toning down the colour a little couldn't hurt" Isabel mused as she continued to eat

Raheem is a little bit strait-laced, he'll probably die when he"

"Who's Raheem?"

"He's a guy from school, we hang out, like, together sometimes"

"WaitYou're dating now?"

The stern tone immediately returned to her mother's voice at this latest revelation. Isabel immediately regretted letting her guard down.

"Is it this, boy, who has you acting out like this?"

"No Mom, it's not like that." Isabel stood as she protested. Hanging out with Raheem has actually calmed things down for Isabel. She hadn't looked forward to going to school for months before he'd asked if he could join her at lunch. He hadn't even been put off by her first, less than friendly, refusal.

Given half a chance, her mother would probably actually approve of Raheem, but there was no way she'd listen now.

"But you're keeping secrets. I thought you'd at least talk to me before you started dating!"

"Dad always said it was better to ask forgiveness than permission!"

"The last thing we need is any advice your father chooses to live by."

"Maybe if you weren't so obsessed with controlling everyone, he'd have stuck around!"

Even in the heat of their argument, Isabel regretted saying that, the moment the words left her lips. An entire spectrum of emotions played across her mother's face. An initial flash of anger quickly gave way to one of sadness, tears welling up in her eyes, and her lower lip beginning to quiver slightly.

"Mom, I"

"Just go to your room."

Her mother spoke in the flat tone of someone teetering on the precipice between enraged screams or floods of tears.

"I didn't"

"NOW!" Her mother snapped, before turning her back on Isabel and returning to the dishes.

"Fine." Isabel muttered, stomping out of the kitchen and upstairs to her room, strategically slamming the bedroom door behind her. Throwing herself face down on the bed, she screamed all of her frustrations with her mother, the rain outside, and her own stupid short fuse, into her pillow.

Catching her breath and rolling onto her side, Isabel clicked the play button on her stereo.

Her mom would likely hate this musicIsabel reached over and cranked the volume upwards several notches.

After a few moments, staring aimlessly at her bedroom ceiling, Isabel sat up determinedly. Shitty rain or no she was going to head out to see Raheem. Not getting to see him all week while he'd been off sick had been lame. Not that she'd tell him that, of course. *Play it cool Issy*, she reminded herself. Still, she couldn't help but grin, imagining his face when he got a look at her new hair.

Getting ready would be easy, pretty much everything Isabel would need was in her room. Pulling on her boots over her skinny black jeans and lacing them tightly, she stood. *No risk of blowing over in the wind wearing these bad boys*, she thought as she opened her closet to retrieve her jacket. Leather wasn't the best choice for the weather, but no way was she turning up to throw stones at her boyfriend's window in a bright yellow waterproof.

Catching her reflection in the mirror, she pulled on her jacket and admired herself. No wonder her mom was worried what the town busybodies would say—she looked like a total badass!

"Hey Raheem!" She rehearsed while raising her eyebrows flirtatiously at her own reflection.

"Come on out—the Water's fine" No good! She didn't really want to stay outside."Gonna invite me in?" No. Too Vampire.

"Yo, Sicknote! Got sick of waiting for *you* to turn up at *my* window..." Perfect!

Next would come the tricky part—actually getting out of the house tonight would be tough, even if mom wasn't pissed off. Isabel flung open her bedroom window and peered into the street below. The rain was still coming down hard, feeding, now free flowing streams, as the drains struggled to deal with the sheer volume of water. Looking out across the road, she unexpectedly noticed two figures outside, braving in the storm. The two people were carrying something between them, though at this distance Isabel couldn't quite make out what it was. She did recognize the people though: she'd know that perfect little daddy's girl Valerie Townsend at 100 paces and—unless there's another kid in town that wears that same jacket every day without fail—that person with her must be Jamie from her math class. Now that was an odd couple if she'd ever seen one. Given the age gap between the unusual pair, she could only guess that, maybe Valerie was tutoring Jamie on being a prissy little loser so he could spend less time in detention. It would be just Valerie to get involved with some try-hard, big-sister program for gold stars and attention.

Isabel turned her focus to the ground below. It wasn't until considering attempting to jump out, that she really noticed how tall houses actually were. Her first thought was making a rope out of her bed sheets, like on TV, to climb down. A few minutes of failing to transform a rectangular sheet into a long rope soon put an end to this idea.

If I climb out backwards and lower myself carefully with my arms, it probably isn't that much of a drop really, she rationalized. *Plus, the ground is probably softened up from all of the rain, and worst case if I break something it'll be mom's fault, and she'll feel terrible about that fight she started.*

In preparation for her great escape, and as a test, Isabel crammed a few essentials into a backpack. A small umbrella, four cans a beer she'd stashed in her cupboard, Walkman and mixtape, eyeliner, and some issues of Creepshow she'd promised Raheem he could borrow. Leaning out of the window Isabel aimed for the driveway and let the bag drop.

SMASH.

The falling backpack shattered a plant pot which sat directly under Isabel's window, spilling waterlogged soil across the ground.

Ok, I'll drop down a little to the left Isabel thought as she hoisted herself on the window ledge, the rain blowing into her face as the wind blew it under the eaves of their house.

Wait—this was crazy. Isabel came to a sudden realisation as she felt the force of the raindrops hitting her skin.

If her hair was going to stand up to this weather, she'd need more hairspray.

Scrambling back into her bedroom, Isabel reached for a can of maximum strength hairspray. Finding the first can in its death throes, she discarded it, grabbed a fresh one and began applying liberally to fortify her new look against the rain.

Her storm proof styling was cut short abruptly as with a sudden cracking sound she found herself plunged simultaneously into darkness and silence...

The power had gone out. Another glance into the street, revealed no other lit houses, or even streetlights. The whole street, if not the town had just gone dark. Fumbling for her bedside cabinet in the pitch black, Isabel's hand first found her dad's old zippo lighter which she'd kept after he'd left. She'd hidden it from her mom, who'd thrown out most of his other things shortly after it became clear he wasn't coming back. Flicking the cover open Isabel thumbed the striking wheel but, remembering the cloud of flammable chemicals she was currently enveloped in a haze of she thought better of it, pocketed the lighter and reached back into the drawer to retrieve a torch.

It wasn't particularly powerful, but the small disc of light the torch projected was better than nothing. Certainly enough to go downstairs and grab some candles, before her mother came to check on her. Lucky she hadn't jumped already.

From nowhere, an almighty crash, seemed to shake the house, startling Isabel and causing her to drop her torch onto her bedroom floor, it landed with a thud, before bouncing and rolling under the bed.

"Shit!" Isabel cursed, instinctively dropping to her hands and knees to retrieve her only source of light. As she stretched to reach under the bed, another sound grabbed her attention as a scream pierced through the sound of the falling rain from outside.

"Mom!?" Grabbing the torch, Isabel sprang back to her feet and bolted out of her room, heavy boots thumping out a dull rhythm on the floorboards as she ran back down to the kitchen. Torch gripped in one hand, and hairspray still clenched in the other.

"Mom!" Isabel shouted louder this time as she reached the kitchen door, as she pushed it open the feeling of the cold and wet hit her before she'd even fully opened it.

"Issy, stay back!"

The kitchen was a ruin. It was like the storm had invited itself inside, shattering the patio doors and littering every surface with broken glass, crockery and leaves blown in from outdoors. Everything was already soaked by the invading weather.

Isabel's torchlight found her mother first, eyes wide with fear, backed against the kitchen cabinets with a knife clutched in one hand. Blood cascaded down one side of her face from a gash at her hairline. Not speaking, she motioned for Isabel to back away as she pointed her knife threateningly at the figure standing at the opposite side of the, now overturned kitchen table. The man, who had his back turned to Isabel, despite a hunched posture was tall, dressed in a long black coat, slick with rain that glinted in the light. In shock, Isabel's grip on the hairspray can loosened, leading it to slip from her grasp and clatter loudly to the floor.

The figure spun in response fixed its gaze on Isabel. Whatever the intruder was, it was clearly no man. The creature's large black eyes showed no reaction to the light, with no pupils to dilate. Isabel stood petrified in the doorway, as, whatever this was cocked its head as it observed her.

The creature gave a series of quiet chirps, disbursed with an occasional clicking as it tapped its feet on the tiled kitchen floor and snapped, a black beak-like mouth. Moving slowly forwards, towards Isabel a clawed hand, silently and ominously emerged from the dark, wet cloak which covered the creature's body and slowly reached towards her.

"Get away from her!" Isabel's mother screamed, launching herself onto the creature's back, bringing the knife down, into its front just below the right shoulder.

Crying in pain, the creature threw back its head as it loosed an awful scream. The sound was a mixture of a woman's cry the caw of a crow and a blender full of loose change. Isabel clapped her hands to her ears to shield them from the awful sound, as her mother pulled the knife free. Before she could strike again however, the creature unfurled, what Isabel had taken as some kind of cloak, revealing them to be an enormous set of black, feathered wings, throwing Isabel's mother into the remains of the kitchen table, snapping an upturned leg with the force of the impact. It's body now uncovered; Isabel could make out more of the more human, surprisingly feminine shaped figure that had been hidden by the wings. Unlike the slick dark feathers of the wings, these inner feathers were softer and lighter, more like fur or down. It was an uncanny sight, not entirely animal or human.

Turning, the creature began to stalk towards her

mother. Isabel reacted, grabbing the first thing she could lay her hands on, a large frying pan. She began desperately striking the invading monster as she screamed. The creature seemed to shrug off the first few hits but following a second to the back of the head it turned and swiped at Isabel with a clawed hand, knocking the pan from her grasp. With a short screech the creature flapped its wings towards Isabel, the force knocking her backwards and onto the floor, before turning its attention back to her mom as she struggled to stand.

Lying on the floor, winded and gasping to refill her lungs, Isabel's hand felt something familiar, as the dropped can of hairspray rolled into reach. With a sudden thought, Isabel gripped the can and leapt up, her free hand rummaging in her pocket for the lighter. Wasting no time, she shook, the hairspray in one hand striking the lighter with the other.

"Hey, Big Bird!"

Before the creature could turn fully, Isabel pressed her finger down on the nozzle of the hairspray can, unleashing a jet of flame directly into its face.

Screaming, the creature began to thrash around, the downy feathers adorning its body beginning to catch and sustain the fire. The creature made an attempt to fly, but had no room to do so, a flap of it wings sending it crashing into the ceiling and showering Isabel in plaster dust.

"Issy, Run!" Her mother panted as she steadied herself, before launching into a full body tackle at the creature, knife slashing. Before Isabel could react and step back however, the flailing creature's wing swung downward, right into her, sending hear sprawling back-wards into the kitchen cabinets. She hit her head—hard.

Isabel's ears rang and she struggled to focus as she cradled her head. Disoriented and confused, she could faintly make out the muffled sound of her mother, scuffling with the creature, maybe calling her. Somewhere, the dropped torch was being knocked around on the floor sending shadows spinning around the room before it settled pointing directly into Isabel's eyes.

Dragging herself back to a sitting position, Isabel looked across the room to see the creature limping out of the destroyed back door into the garden dragging her, now still, mother.

Gathering all of her remaining energy Isabel picked up the torch and half ran half staggered outside after the creature. With one final screech, it opened its wings once again. Now not limited by being indoors, it took to the air with Isabel's mother lying limply in its arms.

Its flight was slow and unsteady, the creature hadn't come out of the fight unscathed, but now it was getting away with her mom.

Isabel took a deep breath and gave chase.

4

RAHEEM

L oading the film into the camera by candlelight
would have been easy for Raheem's Momif she
were still here.

She would have praised her son's attempts with a
smile before taking the camera body from him, deftly
feeding the film roll into the chamber, snapping it shut,
and passing it back with one hand while ruffling his hair
with the other. She probably could've done it with her
eyes closed. Blindfolded too. And standing on one leg.

But Mom was dead, and her favourite camera had
grown thick with dust until Raheem had rescued it from
her old things this morning and brought it to his
bedroom.

Perhaps now he could get his Dad to listen to him.

Raheem dropped the camera onto his bed and
grabbed another Kleenex. All this crying wasn't helping
his head cold. He blew his nose and dropped the used
tissue into the growing mountain of them at his feet.
Mom would have tidied these away by now, and have a

mug of something hot on his bedside table. She'd read to him until he fell asleep.

The wind rattled his window and threatened to blow out the only candle still burning on his desk.

There had been no power since yesterday. The storm that everyone said would pass had now reached such ferocity that it was holding people prisoner inside their own homes. This fact should've made Raheem feel better about being stuck home from school all week, but dusk was now falling on Creekwood Pines and after dark *it* would come back.

The creature had visited every night this week. He'd seen it that first nightheard it every night since.

Dad wouldn't listen though. 'It's only the wind,' was what he had said. But Raheem was starting to doubt every word that came out his father's mouth these days. He hadn't been the same since Mom's passing. He'd taken on more work and was rarely home. Family meals were missed regularly. And parts of the house were kept strictly off-limits. Dad wouldn't even sleep in their bedroom anymoremost nights Raheem would hear him wailing on the sofa.

His father was there now. Raheem could hear him even over the storm.

Raheem distracted himself again with the camera. If the winged creature returned tonight, then they were both in danger. If he could just snap a photograph of it then maybe his Dad might finally believe him. Raheem had ransacked his Mom's encyclopedia collection to find some mention of the bird-like beast he'd seen in the sky that first night but nothing in the ornithology section even came close. He'd almost given up hope when a drawing had caught his eye on an unlikely page...

Under 'Ancient Myths'.

Raheem felt a surge of excitement as the film spool finally slotted into the camera and snapped shut.

Just as he heard his father's sobbing stop dead.

"Dad?" he said, looping the camera strap around his neck and approaching his bedroom door. "You okay?"

He strained to listen as the storm continued to batter the house. His door groaned as he stepped out into the dark hallway. "Dad, answer if you can hear me."

Raheem felt something reach up and brush his stomach. He let out a scream and swatted at it

His Mom's camera.

He laughed at himself. The darkness had him spooked. He forced himself to take a slow, deep breath. Instead of feeling his way downstairs he could use this.

Ka-shick!

The momentary flash blinded Raheem... but it was just enough for him to get his bearings. He took a few tentative steps out onto the landing and raised the camera again.

Ka-shick!

Raheem found the staircase and carefully began to descend, taking each step one at a time. The noise from each stair sounded like thunder. He suddenly felt very exposed, as if something might be hanging above him in the blackness. He raised the camera, but fear stopped his finger and he lowered it again.

Eventually he reached the bottom step. He had walked this path a million times but now, in the pitch black with his heart rate rising, he couldn't decide where to turn. He shakily raised the camera.

Ka-shick!

His father was standing right in front of him.

The shock sent Raheem back on his heels and he fell sprawling onto the staircase.

"Son?"

Raheem flashed the camera again to make sure that his eyes weren't playing tricks on him.

Ka-shick!

His father's eyes were red. "Is that your mother's camera?"

He heard his father walk across the hallway, open a drawer, and pull something out. There was a rattle and he heard the strike of a match. The room was thrown into sharp relief.

His father passed the candle to him while lighting another for himself. Raheem peeled himself up off the stairs. "You okay, Dad?"

A vein throbbed in his father's forehead. He looked like he was about to burst. But something in him deflated, like air leaking from a burst balloon. He sagged before him.

"C'mon," his father said. "Let's get you something to eat."

They walked by candlelight into the kitchen and Raheem sat at the counter. His Dad walked around to the refrigerator which was leaking a puddle of water onto the tiled floor. His feet splashed as he opened the door and an almighty stink wafted out into the room. "On second thoughts," he said, closing it with a grimace, "Maybe I can find something in the—"

Raheem was suddenly aware of a presence in the corner of the room. Something very, *very* big. Before his mind could fully register the shock, the thing moved. Fast.

A scream rocked the fridge, extinguishing both candles and casting the room back into darkness.

His father's voice came from somewhere low to the ground, he'd fallen to the floor. "What the hell was that? Raheem? Are you alright, son?"

Raheem shushed him. He couldn't see but something about the quality of the air told him that the intruder was still here with them. The stink was even worse now; like wet dog and rancid meat. In his gut he knew that it was the creature from the sky he'd seen a few nights ago. He'd heard its screeching every night and now it had finally come for him. The winged beast from his mother's books.

Raheem heard the rattle of the matchbox as his father quickly lit up another candle, still lying on the ground.

"Dad, no!"

But it was too late. All at once, the kitchen was bathed in the orange glow of the candle's tiny flame—which might as well have been a spotlight trained on his father. Raheem's eye was drawn to the ceiling where the black mass clung. It howled—a strange mix of a woman's scream and birdsong—as it dropped to the floor and stood to its full height before him. It turned to his father on the floor and took one heavy step towards him on taloned feet.

It hated the fire.

Seeing it close up, Raheem realised that his worst fears were correct: He'd failed to find a match in his mother's books because this was no creature borne from nature

This was something borne out of a nightmare.

The black feathered creature towered above him. An inhuman trill escaped its beak-like maw. Huge terrible wings sprouted from its back, enveloping a delicate woman's body. Raheem felt bile rise in his throat as he realized that he was both repulsed and aroused when the bird-woman's wings parted to reveal a scorched but naked torso inside; its sagging breasts swaying as it lumbered towards his father's prone body.

"Raheem, RUN!"

Miraculously, his Dad had sprung to his feet and was now rushing towards him. He grabbed Raheem and pulled him towards the back door. They burst through it, exploding out from the dark house and into a hurricane.

Or at least that's how it felt. Raheem had forgotten all about the storm but now he was being buffeted on all sides by the ferocious wind. He didn't look back as they ran around the house towards the street. His father had his arm around him, shielding him from the worst of the foul weather. Running blind, Raheem could barely open his eyes when he heard the terrible sound that had haunted him all week.

It had followed them outside.

With a squawk, the shadow slashed at them with a vicious swipe. They fell as one, hitting tarmac, and Raheem felt heavy thuds through the protection of his father's body as the creature thrashed at him again and again. His dad screamed as Raheem squeezed out from under him and stood next to the two struggling bodies.

He didn't hesitate. He lunged, grabbing the coarse

feathers on the creature's back. He tugged on the black shape, but it was useless. The thing was too large and Raheem too slight. He beat his fists on it uselessly as he heard his father's screams fade into the storm with each passing second. If only he could see what he was doing! In the dim moonlight he could make out shapes—it was like wrestling a phantom.

Of course.

His mother's camera was still around his neck. He grabbed it, pointed it at the huge bird, and pressed the shutter.

Ka-shick!

The flash was like a gunshot.

All at once, the scene before him came into view. His father's body on the street, bloody and torn to ribbons. The bird-woman above him, dazed and screaming at the explosion of light. He heard her fall backwards, away from his father. The camera flash *hurt* her. Emboldened by this realisation, Raheem stepped over his father and kept clicking, driving the beast back.

Ka-shick! Ka-shick! Ka-shick!

The thing retreated. And with every blinding flash the hideous woman's face winced and grew fearful. Its claws sounded like knives on the asphalt as it reached the kerb and stumbled, blind and screaming. With a final *ka-shick!* he saw the beast spread its wings and take flight into the night sky. It shot straight up and disappeared into the black clouds.

When he was sure the creature had gone, he ran to his father.

His Dad's wide eyes scanned the heavens. "What was that thing?"

Raheem knew. He'd tried to tell him but now hardly felt the time for an 'I-told-you-so.' "Shh, don't talk," he said, wiping his runny nose with his sleeve and examining his father's injuries.

Bruises were beginning to bloom on his Dad's body. His clothes were ripped, and his skin was covered in hundreds of tiny cuts. But thankfully the wounds weren't too deep. The bleeding had already stopped. His father might be out of action for a long timebut he'd live. He couldn't bear the thought of losing another parent.

The old man tried to sit up, but Raheem gently pushed him back. "You need to rest."

"It'll take more than—*whatever that thing was*—to keep me down," he joked, his laugh turning to a painful, racking cough and then a groan. "I'm fine, I'm fine."

His father tried to sit up again but fell back to the ground, his eyes rolling back into his head. Raheem felt hot tears begin to formwhen his Dad let out a snore.

The storm cocooned them. gale force winds swirled fallen leaves and trash around their bodies in a miniature cyclone. For a moment, the creature, the rest of the world none of it mattered—until Raheem heard the sound of footsteps.

He tensed, readying himself for another fight. He set his father down as gently as he could and picked up a stick that had blown nearby. He held it like a baseball bat and turned towards the sound.

A shadow emerged from the night. Followed by another, then another.

Raheem had been about to knock them senseless but he let the stick fall to his side. "Jamie? Valerie? *Teen Wolf?*"

It was his friends from school: Jamie. And Valerie

Townsend. Perhaps the last two people he ever expected to see together. They were each wearing some sort of body armour except for the third figure who Raheem now recognized as Jamie's little brother, Frank, who had pulled back his miniature Teen Wolf mask to reveal his gap-toothed smile. After the insanity of tonight, Raheem had completely forgotten tomorrow was Halloween.

His friends were holding makeshift weapons of their own; a socket wrench, curling tongs, and a NES Zapper. "What are you guys doing here?" he asked.

Jamie was the first to talk. Raheem saw him notice his Dad's body and grimace. "We saw flashing lights."

The group stood in a circle as the storm continued around them. Jamie was wearing hockey pads and a head torch. Valerie's eyes were watching the street as if she expected something to jump out at any moment. Raheem wanted to hug them both. "You've seen it too?" he asked.

"It's taken our parents. We've been watching for it. Waiting."

Raheem looked down at his father. He was still out cold. "You missed it."

Jamie hung his head. "I'm sorry that we didn't get here sooner."

Raheem realized how this must've looked. "Dad's alive. Just unconscious."

His friend looked up, amazed and relieved.

"I managed to scare it off with this," Raheem continued, holding up the camera. "Doesn't like the flash."

Jamie nodded. "We can use that against it."

Valerie sounded anxious. "But we still don't know what the heck *it* is," she said.

Raheem remembered his Mom's book. He sunk down

on his knees next to his Dad. "I might be able to help with that. Just help me get him inside first."

When they had wrestled his father's body into the house, Raheem ran upstairs to his bedroom and grabbed the encyclopedia from his bedside table. Taking it back down, he had it open to the relevant page before he had reached the last step. "Take a look at this," he said, holding the book open in the middle of the group. It was the Greek Mythology section and he pointed to the page detailing Homer, author of *The Odyssey*. "I saw it a few nights ago: a giant bird in the sky. I couldn't find anything in the bird books, but I did find this." He turned the page, pointing to an illustration that each of the four children now recognized. "They've been written about many times over the centuries. 'Maidens with the bodies of birds.' Whenever a person disappeared, they were said to have been carried off by these creatures."

Valerie's nose almost touched the pages. "What are they?"

Raheem looked into the faces of his friends, "It's a Harpy: spirit with the destructive power of wind."

The group held their collective breathbefore Jamie burst out laughing.

"Yeah, right," he said. "The destructive power of *wind*? Pull the other one, we're not dealing with some ancient fart monster here."

Frank snickered and echoed his big brother's joke, "Fart monster!"

Raheem punched his friend in the arm, "This is serious, Jamie. I'm not kidding around."

Jamie held up his hands and stifled the last of his

giggles. When he had composed himself, he looked around. "Did Isabel make it here?"

Raheem shook his head. "I haven't seen her all week."

Jamie and Valerie looked at each other, all the laughter gone now.

"Guys?"

Valerie reluctantly spoke up. "We heard a commotion at Isabel's last night but by the time we got over there everybody was gone. We hoped that she was with you."

Raheem was speechless. He felt sick. With everything that was going on he hadn't even thought about Isabel once, what kind of boyfriend did that make him? He was about to ask what happened when he realized someone else was missing too. "Where's Frank?" he asked, looking at the child-size wolf mask that lay discarded on the floor.

They searched the house. With each empty room Jamie grew more and more panicked. "It's got him," he said. "The... Harpy, or whatever the hell you want to call it, has got him." Jamie turned to Raheem and grabbed him by the collar. "We've got to go find him. We have to go *now*."

"We will," Raheem pleaded. "But we need a plan. We can't just go running off into the storm without any clue where he might have gone."

"What about these books of yours? Do they tell you where to find a Harpy?"

"No. But we can watch for her. Eventually she's going to show up."

"I'm not waiting."

Raheem understood what his friend was going through. When his Mom had died, he would have run into oncoming traffic if he'd thought there was even a chance to bring her back. This storm wasn't going to stop Jamie. And it shouldn't stop Raheem from finding Isabel either. "Okay," he said at last. "There's just one thing I need to do first."

Raheem walked back through to where his father lay and removed the film from the camera. He only required the flash anyway and there was something on this roll of film that his Dad needed to see. He placed the spool into his father's hand. "Maybe now you'll believe me," he said, kissing him on the forehead and walking quickly back to his friends before he might start crying.

He found them at the front door. Something was on the other side.

Jamie raised his wrench; Valerie, her tongs; Raheem, his stick.

They watched the door handle slowly turn.

It burst open with all the force of the storm outside.

Isabel stood there, drenched with muck and blood. Only the whites of her eyes shone out from the darkness and she was breathing hard. "Guys," she said. "I need your help... I know where the nest is."

5

THE NEST

"Jamie, I really wish you'd let me drive, I at least have my learners permit."

What Valerie said made perfect sense, but Jamie needed to feel like he was in control of something. First his mom had been taken, and now Frank too.

"Don't worry Val, I drive my Mom's car all the time. I've got this."

Jamie wouldn't dream of admitting aloud that his driving experiences were solely from bringing his mom's car back from Shelly's when her drinking had first started to get bad. These drives had only been a couple of blocks, and never in weather like this.

The car crawled along. Rain lashed mercilessly against the windscreen. Jamie poked at the interior controls in vain hope that the wipers had some, previously hidden, faster setting, capable of keeping up and making it easier to see anything up ahead.

"If anything, I should be driving. It's my Dad's car after all." Raheem chimed in from the back seat.

"No offence bud, but with you driving, your plan to wait until sunrise would have happened, whether we'd all agreed or not."

They were all tired, half of them were nursing injuries and they'd spent the last couple of hours cobbling together weapons and equipment ready to raid the location Isabel insisted the creature was nesting and, more importantly, taking their family members.

A few hours spent sleeping, applying better first aid and hoping the storm eased up were all sensible ideas, but that thing had snatched his brother, and the faster Jamie could get to him, the better the chances of him coming home alive.

Jamie glanced at the LCD clock, glowing with orange numbers on the dashboard. 3:17AM. Frank had been gone for about four hours. Was that already too long? Adjusting the rear-view mirror, he turned his attention to the final member of the party in the back of the car. Isabel was rummaging through her backpack, taking stock of the items she'd brought along.

"You going to insist you should be driving to complete the set?" Jamie scoffed.

"Dude! I've been awake for god knows how long and almost definitely have a concussion. You go for it," Isabel insisted.

"Isabel, you're sure you saw the thing land at school?" Valerie asked.

"Well, now you mention it, maybe I was confused, and it was actually the mall." Isabel returned sarcastically before continuing. "I'm sure I saw it land on the roof edge with my Mom, it was strutting around screeching for a bit and then it disappeared. The place is boarded up tight so I couldn't get in, but I watched for a couple of hours and I didn't see it fly off anywhere else.

"So, our school is a monster nest? Figures." Jamie muttered.

"Harpy!" Raheem corrected. "I'm certain it's a Harpy, the weird mix of bird and woman. This weird storm, it's certainly mean enough."

"If it's a Harpy, does that make us Argonauts?" Isabel asked with a slight smile.

"Argo-what?" Valerie queried.

"Jamie and the Argonauts does have something of a ring to it," Jamie quickly added.

For a fleeting few moments, the surreal situation, the panic and worry dissolved, and the group erupted into playful bickering about who was the leader of the mismatched group. Their fears momentarily forgotten in a cacophony of laughter.

Jamie turned a final corner and the group fell silent once again. The car's high beams illuminated a familiar building up ahead. A few moments later, they bumped up the curb.

"We're here," Jamie said.

THE SCHOOL'S MAIN ENTRANCE BURST OPEN, AND THE group spilled in out of the rain, scattering themselves and their belongings across the hall floor.

Valerie threw her jacket to the floor, wiped the rain from her face and re-tied her hair into a tight ponytail before seeing how the others were doing.

Raheem and Isabel were together at the other side of the hall. Jamie leaned against the wall just inside the school entrance, the bolt cutters and crowbar he'd used to battle through the chains and boarding used to secure the school discarded around him. Getting in had been harder work and had taken longer than he'd expected, and he was clearly tired from the exertion.

Valerie placed her hand gently on his shoulder as he hunched over.

"Nice job getting us in. Are you alright?" she asked.

"Wish Raheem... would have just... let me drive the car into... the door... like I wanted to," Jamie spoke slowly between deep breaths. "I'll be fine, just need a second."

Valerie decided to give Jamie some space to recover and addressed the others.

"So guys, we're inside, now what?

"We head up," Raheem answered as he and Isabel walked over to join them. Everybody looked up at the discolored ceiling above them.

"The nest is either up on the roof or maybe whatever this place has in the way of attic space. We have to get up there," Isabel explained.

"Ok, so we get up there, hopefully the Harpy is out somewhere, we find our families and get everyone out, right?" Valerie said.

She hoped it would be as simple as that. That it wouldn't be too late for everyone.

"But, if it's there..." Isabel brought up the possibility that Valerie was doing her best to try and ignore.

"Then we kill it!" Jamie brought his recovered crowbar down on a radiator with a clang as he spoke, his previously tired expression replaced by a look of renewed determination.

Valerie shifted the strap of the hunting rifle where it hung across her shoulder. Her dad had taught her to shoot it on a camping trip last summer, when he'd taken a rare day off. Picking up on how to load and shoot the rifle had gone pretty well, but she'd been very clear with her dad that she refused to shoot any living creature. Valerie looked around at the rest of the group as they each examined their own equipment, far more cobbled together and makeshift, with not much else you'd consider an actual weapon. She began to feel a creeping anxiety that the group would be looking to her to make the difference if things got ugly.

"You doing ok Valerie?" Raheem asked.

"Y-Yeah, I'm ready," Valerie confirmed. "No actually, hold on…"

Reaching into her coat pocket Valerie retrieved the birthday present Lesley had given her on the last day before the school had been closed, and her dad had vanished.

"If we die here, at least I'll have celebrated my birthday," she grinned.

She tugged again at the bundle of Sellotape with no success, but this time she wouldn't let it beat her.

"Somebody toss me a knife."

Jamie pulled a penknife from his pocket, unfolded the blade and handed it over. The blade was a little dull, but it was more than enough to make short work of the tape and her gift was finally free. As the paper fell away a smile crossed Valerie's lips.

"What you get?" Jamie shone his torch at the bundle in Valerie's hands.

"It's some permanent markers," she said softly.

"Markers?" Jamie said. "Fat use they are."

Valerie ignored him. "It's silly, really—back when I first made friends with Lesley, my Mom was babysitting for her kid brother. She'd fallen asleep on the sofa, while Lesley and I *actually* hung out with him. He drew on my Mom's face with a marker, glasses, mustache—the lot! We somehow all kept straight faces, until Lesley's Mom came home. She was so angry."

The markers rested on a slab of chocolate: Valerie's favorite kind, too! Pocketing the pens, Valerie held the bar aloft victoriously.

"Share this with me, guys?"

After some faux token protests about not needing to share her birthday present the other three, none of them having had a proper meal for some time, all sat in a circle on the floor of their school's entrance and tucked into the chocolate ravenously. Mumbling thanks and 'Happy Birthday' through mouths full of chewy nougat.

"Hey Val, throw me one of those markers, would you?" Jamie asked.

Obliging, Valerie tossed him one of the markers from her pocket.

"If we don't make it out of this, we should at least leave our mark."

Jamie uncapped the marker and began to draw on the corridor tiles. Understanding, the others signalled for markers and copied his example. Each writing something on the ground in a different color.

Valerie wrote, 'Love you Dad, and If I don't survive, Lesley: thanks for the present,' followed by a smiley face. It was all she could think of in the moment.

Jamie had written simply, 'For my brother'.

Isabel scrawled, 'Victoria Carlsson sez: Principal Weill is a Dork', she explained this was her mom in response to confused looks.

Finally, after some thought, Raheem wrote 'It's just what Mom would have done. Love you Dad' and then a heart shape with R + I inside it, adding an arrow and flames after Isabel had initially teased him for being lame.

"Ok!" Jamie stood back up as he spoke, "Everyone make sure you have everything you need."

Valerie knelt to check her backpack as she heard the distinctive thud of Isabel's heavy boots next to her.

"Hey. Look, I know we've never really got on..." Isabel began.

"It's fine. Can't be friends with everyone right?" Valerie looked up at Isabel with a smile. Not getting on was a slight understatement, she'd been pretty sure Isabel hated her. *Targeted* her, even.

"Nah, it's not really fine. I can be a bit of a bitch some-times... It's just... You seem to have it all: most kids always say hi to you, and your dad is the sheriff he's always looking out for you and I guess I just felt like..." Isabel paused.

In their other (all less pleasant) exchanges Valerie had never seen Isabel struggle for words.

"Isabel, it's fine," Valerie said. "I wish it hadn't taken a mythical creature kidnapping our parents to get us talking but we're here now, and I can't think of anyone else in school I'd rather have with me to fight a monster than you."

"Harpy!" Raheem corrected as he overheard.

"Thanks Valerie. You're alright, y'know," Isabel returned her smile and offered her a hand to stand as Valerie zipped up her backpack. "Now, let's go kill this feathery bitch!"

RAHEEM LED THE WAY AS THE GROUP WALKED CAREFULLY through the school corridors, not wanting to make too much noise this close to the Harpy's lair. It was beyond surreal seeing their school, which they'd all only ever seen crowded with people and well lit, as they did now, dark and abandoned.

Muddy streaks and footprints coated the corridor tiles. It looked like, when they closed the school due to the weather, not even the staff had been allowed in. Either that or they'd fallen victim to the Harpy too.

With a shudder at the thought, Raheem reached his free hand backwards to take Isabel's. She caught his hand and increased her pace to walk alongside him, the contents of her backpack clinking together as she moved.

"How much did you get in the end?" Raheem asked.

"Managed to fill two and a half jars of gasoline from the can in your dad's shed," Isabel explained. Had to tip your pickles down the toilet to empty the jars though. Sorry."

"Don't worry. At least you backed down on your idea

to fill Frank's water gun with gasoline, you'd have burned your face off."

Isabel gave an exaggerated look of horror.

"You're saying you wouldn't be into me anymore if I burned my face? You're just like all the other boys!"

"Hmmm, well…" Raheem continued. "Would you still at least have that awesome hair?"

She squeezed his hand a little tighter. They were silent for a second.

"You think fire will kill it?" Raheem added.

"Fire kills everything. I'd have roasted old Jamie-Lee-Bird-Tits back at my house had it not gotten outside into the rain. This time we have better fuel and rope to hold it down. Plus, Valerie has her dad's rifle and then there's… well, there's your camera."

Now, it was Raheem's turn to give an exaggerated hurt look as he cradled his mom's old camera.

"This camera saved us back at my house. It doesn't seem to like the flash. I'm guessing its eyes are probably better in the dark. Or maybe, as it's always flying in that storm, it imagines that the bright flashes are lightning, and it doesn't want to be near that."

"Solid theories, doc. I knew I wasn't just with you for your looks," Isabel grinned.

As the group moved up to the second floor of the school building, the effects of the weather became more obvious. Dark patches of damp could be seen bleeding from the ceiling, there were leaks in the roof. Raheem took a deep breath through his nose, as he tried to identify the smell. There was an unpleasant odor in the air, like rot and festering food, he'd smelled something a little similar once when their freezer had broken in the summer and all of the food in there had gone bad.

"There's a maintenance room up by the lockers, guys, I reckon that that's where the attic access will be," Raheem spoke in a stage whisper. He had a feeling that they were getting close.

The lockers were just up ahead, along with a wooden door labelled 'Staff Only'. It was locked, of course, but before Raheem could even draw breath to ask, Jamie went at it with his crowbar. Unlike the external doors, this old door wasn't intended to keep anything more than nosy kids out. The old wood and locking mechanism bent to the iron will of the crowbar and the door swung open. The group stood in the entryway, their torch beams searching the ceiling.

Jackpot!

"How do we get up there?" Valerie was the first to notice the lack of any type of ladder in the storeroom.

"Shit! Frank doesn't have time for this," Jamie was clearly frustrated with the idea of being so close, only to find another barrier in front of them.

Isabel stepped forward, "Somebody give me a boost!"

ISABEL SLUNG HER TORCH INTO THE ATTIC AHEAD OF HER. The attic was crowded with wooden support beams but was large enough for her to stand at full height. It was the smell that hit her first—the stench of rotten roadkill almost made her gag.

Steadying herself she continued further into the attic. Up ahead, she could make out a large hole in the roof, rain pouring in as the storm continued to rage outside. There was something else to the side of the opening, a large pile of something she couldn't identify.

Swallowing her nerves, she edged forward, checking the kitchen knife was still safely tucked into her belt.

With a squeal, the walkie talkie Jamie had given her sprang to life and almost made her jump out of her skin.

"Isabel. You ok?" Raheem's voice came through, slightly distorted.

"Dude, I've been gone 30 seconds!" Isabel hissed back into the device.

"Valerie and Jamie have gone to grab tables and chairs from one of the classrooms, we'll be up as soon as we can," Raheem explained. "Do you see anything?"

"There's something up ahead. I'm going to check it out."

"Be careful."

"When am I ever?"

Isabel left it at that and continued forward. As she approached, the floorboards began to grow sticky, coated in a matted mess of feathers and gunk. The pile she'd seen from the attic entrance was a huge tangle of branches and other debris, all stacked together and coated in more of the feathery mess, it looked like a bird's nest.

With a sudden sense of vulnerability, Isabel shone her torchlight around the nest itself in a panicked and frantic search for the Harpy. Thankfully, there was no sign of it.

While focussing her attention upwards, Isabel had neglected to watch her feet and she stepped on something that shattered and crunched under her boot.

Glancing down, Isabel saw the remains of what might have once been a rodent or small cat, the whole floor was littered with bones and other remains, the pile of carcasses growing thicker as she got closer to the nest itself.

Isabel was about to reach back for the radio when she noticed something that stopped her in her tracks.

A mass of bizarre cocoons were lined up at the base of the nest. They were all made of the same sticky gunge that seemed to coat everything up here. Some of the smaller ones contained decomposing animals, but there were larger ones too. Isabel shone her light on the closest pod.

Valerie's father was inside.

"Guys! I've found them!" Isabel shouted into the radio.

Raheem replied, but the sound of scrambling from the hatch was enough indication that the others were on their way. As they climbed up, Isabel frantically examined the other cocoons to find that there were several adults she didn't know. Based on the hair color, the second one could have been Jamie's mom. In the sixth, she finally found her.

"Mom?!"

Her mother was warm, but unconscious, her breathing was shallow. No matter what Isabel did she couldn't rouse her.

She continued shaking, calling and even slapping her mom to wake her. The others ran up behind her, all joining in the attempts to raise their loved ones with similar success.

"There's something wrong with them," Raheem

commented. "Not sure if it's a chemical in whatever they're all bundled in or something else, but there's no waking them up."

Valerie ran over to her Dad. "Oh, thank God."

"My best guess is that she's keeping them asleep and... well, fresh." Raheem spoke gravely, casting torch-light on the scattered bones on the ground to illustrate his point.

"Frank! Where's Frank?" Jamie cut in, desperately searching the pods in vain for his missing brother.

"I don't see him here," Valerie joined Jamie in his frantic search efforts.

"Guys!" As the others turned in response to Isabel's shout, she pointed silently into the very centre of the nest.

There, sleeping soundly, not in a cocoon, but on a soft mound of feathers, lay Frank.

Jamie rushed the nest to reach his brother but before he'd taken a second step—

Screech!

Everyone froze, the blood turning to ice in their veins.

Screech!

"Oh shit," Raheem uttered.

"Everybody get ready," Jamie ordered.

"The bitch is back!" Isabel yelled.

Screech!

Jamie shouldered his crowbar, Raheem primed his camera flash, Isabel grabbed a jar of gasoline from her backpack and Valerie clicked off the safety on her dad's rifle.

The Harpy swooped through the hole in the roof, landing with an almighty crash, scattering bones and entrails it had left scattered around the attic. It eyed the group of intruders and lurched towards them.

The group split up.

JAMIE KILLED HIS LIGHT AND LOOKED BACK TOWARDS THE nest from his hiding place behind one of the attic's support struts. One of the others must have dropped their torch as it now lay on the floor, illuminating the Harpy as it inspected the nest for any damage. Feeling his heart thumping against his ribcage he tightened his grip on the crowbar and hoped the others all remembered the plan. He closed his eyes and fought to steady his breathing. Frank and his mom both needed him now, more than ever.

Satisfied, that both her larder and her hostage remained in the nest, the Harpy turned and let out a different sound to the screeches they'd heard previously. This was a gentler, almost cooing call, it was like the Harpy was trying to coax them out of hiding. Jamie thought back to some of Raheem's theories on what the creature wanted, he then thought about Frank being laid gently in the nest and the care package of bugs left at his house. Did this monster consider them children?

A shrill mechanical wail from across the attic, cut through the air and Jamie's train of thought—it was now or never!

The Harpy rushed towards the sound without any hesitation, straight past Jamie's hiding place, leaving a route to the nest unguarded.

"Hope you've got this, guys"

He bolted towards the nest; crowbar ready.

THE HARPY SHRIEKED AND CONFUSEDLY STARED AT THE PAIR of Walkie-Talkies screaming electronic feedback in protest of having been taped together. Not knowing what to make of the squealing devices at first, the Harpy screeched and snapped its beak at in an attempt to elicit some kind of response. Finally, it brought its talons down and smashed the walkie-talkies into a wreck of silent components.

Right in the centre of the noose.

"Pull!" Raheem bellowed

The snare tightened around the Harpy's foot before the creature could react—they had it!

Raheem leapt from his hiding place, camera raised.

Ka-shick.

Ka-shick.

Ka-shick.

Each flash sent the Harpy reeling backwards, The creature was dazzled. It lashed out blindly in Raheem's direction. Raheem leapt back to avoid the confused attack but kept triggering the flash the moment it charged, he needed to keep the Harpy's attention.

ISABEL STEPPED OUT FROM THE DARKNESS BEHIND THE Harpy, she'd need to act fast.

She discarded the lid of the first jar and flung as much gasoline over the Harpy's back and wings as she could. Retrieving the second jar from under her arm Isabel repeated the dousing, this time also trying to get more of the fuel around the creature's legs and onto the floor beneath it.

Sensing it was surrounded, the Harpy snapped backwards at Isabel, forcing her to jump away from its maw.

Isabel slipped on a bone fragment and landed with a hard whump on the floor.

"Hey!" Raheem shouted, trying to wrestle the Harpy's attention back to him, but with repeated uses the flash had begun to lose its dazzling effect. Shaking its head, the creature glared down at Isabel as it towered over her.

At this distance she could see the scorched feathers and seared flesh from their last encounter. She wondered if it remembered her.

The looming Harpy opened its black wings wide, the feathers gleamed in the scattered torchlight as fuel dripped from them.

BANG!

A shot rang out across the attic as an explosion of blood erupted from the Harpy's right knee. Isabel covered her face.

"Nice shot, Valerie!" Raheem shouted.

The creature cried in pain and slumped forwards, trying to steady itself on the other leg to avoid toppling over.

Isabel pulled her dad's lighter from her pocket and caught the Harpy's eye as she struck the wheel to summon the flames.

"Watch the birdie," she taunted.

Flames engulfed the Harpy, the ferocious roar of the fire almost drowning out its pained screams as both

Raheem and Isabel scrambled away towards where Valerie was standing, rifle still raised.

The creature thrashed desperately against the rope that held it in place, erratically thrashing around and coated in fire, it looked like the devil's own personal kite. The three stood, watching as it burned. Intense heat radiated around the attic.

Raheem had earned himself a few scratches from his close encounter, and Isabel nursed her hand where it looked like the flames had caught her, but they were just minor injuries.

"You should shoot it again," Raheem said quietly as the struggles and cries began to die down. "Finish it off."

Nodding, Valerie took aim.

With a sudden, final surge of desperate strength, the Harpy flung itself forwards through the air towards the group of children. The rope, damaged by the flames, gave way and snapped.

Valerie pulled the trigger in panic, but in her haste she missed. The bullet flew harmlessly to lodge somewhere into the attic wall. The Harpy barrelled into them.

JAMIE SPRINTED TOWARDS THE GROUP JUST IN TIME TO SEE the Harpy snatch Valerie and crash blindly into several of the support beams holding up the school roof near the existing opening.

Looking on helplessly, he felt his heart sink as the struts splintered and shattered with the force of the impact bringing another large section of the roof collapsing down onto both the Harpy and, more importantly, Valerie. The flames began to extinguish, hungrily eating through the Harpy's wings and caught by the rain which poured through the broken roof.

Raheem and Isabel had been knocked aside in the attack and were struggling back to their feet.

Jamie had broken everyone out of the cocoons and pulled Frank out of the nest, but he still hadn't been able to wake them up. He hoped that they would return to consciousness in time.

He looked through the clouds of dust kicked up by the collapse looking for any sign of Valerie, and then he saw her, lying prone at the feet of the Harpy. Its feathers were now pretty much all gone, and its wings were twisted bald ruins, but somehow it was still standing.

His fears, worries, and anxiety all disappeared in an instant, all replaced by a burning rage that consumed Jamie from head to toe.

The Harpy's own screech was drowned out when Jamie roared and raced through the attic towards the monster, crowbar in one hand, kitchen knife in the other.

As soon as he was within reach Jamie plunged the knife into the Harpy's chest. The skin, already blistered and burned, erupted with black blood oozing from every cut he made—but it still didn't go down.

Bloody, clawed hands seized Jamie by the waist and lifted him off the ground until he was eye to eye with the beast.

With a screech, the Harpy dug its beak into Jamie's chest. It burned and stole his breath as the razor-sharp beak gouged into him. The world seemed to shrink, and he heard the knife clink as it hit the floor.

With one final scream of "DIE!", Jamie raised the

crowbar and plunged it into the creature's eye. He felt some resistance, but kept pushing, forcing the bar deeper into its skull.

The Harpy, gurgled, grunted and threw its head back with a hideous scream. It began to topple backwards as its grip on Jamie loosened. They both fell.

IT WAS DARK FOR A WHILE. JAMIE WAS LESS AWARE OF THE pain in his chest now, but couldn't bring himself to move.

"Jamie? Jamie! Wake up!"

Forcing his eyes open he saw Valerie, covered in cuts and dust but alive. Raheem and Isabel arrived and gathered around him too, cradling his injured body.

"Hey guys," he managed weakly. "Is it..."

"Yeah, it's dead," Isabel finished, "You killed it."

"No, we killed it," Jamie corrected her.

"Just hang in there, buddy." Raheem had taken hold of his hand and squeezed it tightly.

Jamie, fought to keep his eyes open, he was suddenly very tired.

"Jamie!"

A voice called from the other side of the attic. He'd know that voice anywhere.

"Frank," Jamie managed. A smile crossed his lips as he collapsed back into darkness.

FRANK LAY FRUSTRATED IN THE HOSPITAL BED. HE, AND ALL the other victims of the nest, felt fine as soon as they'd woken up, but the sheriff and the doctors had made everyone who'd been witness to the night's events stay in the hospital for an extra few days while they ran their tests.

He supposed it wasn't too bad; the doctors had said he was allowed ice cream with his dinner if he behaved.

"Hey, squirt!"

Jamie's friends were at the door to his room, his mother standing behind them in her hospital gown. They'd visited each other a lot since he'd been in hospital and he hoped they'd still get to hang out after he got home.

Raheem gave him his own walkie talkie so he could join in their radio talks, and Valerie said he could come to one of their horror movie nights.

Isabel gave him a dead arm for making fun of her hair, but she was ok, too.

When, a short time later, the guys left, his mom waited behind.

"Frank, sweetie. I know I haven't been the best at looking after you and your brother these last few months. I promise that I'm going to do better, okay?"

"Ok, Mom." Frank smiled

"The doctors say you're allowed to go home today," she added. "I'm going to go and see them quickly, get your stuff ready to go. Your brother will need to stay here a little longer, but if we're quiet, we can visit with him quickly before we go home"

After his mom left, Frank leapt out of his bed and rushed to his backpack. Opening the zip, he stared at the egg, which felt warm and delicate in his hands. His plan to keep it safe, wrapped in his clothes, had been working.

He still couldn't quite believe that no one else had seen the little black oval in the nest.

He rubbed a hand gently along its curves. When he had found it, he knew the adults would never have let him keep it if they knew, so he just hid it in his bag. He'd soon find a warm, safer spot to raise it back at home.

ABOUT DANIEL WILLCOCKS

Daniel Willcocks is an Amazon best-selling author and podcaster of dark fiction. He is one fifth of digital story studio, Hawk & Cleaver, co-producer of iTunes-busting 'The Other Stories' podcast, as well as the lead host of the Great Writers Share' podcast. Residing in the UK, Dan's work explores the catastrophic and the strange. Find out more at www.danielwillcocks.com

ABOUT BEN ERRINGTON

Ben Errington: With debut novel 'Ten Tales of the Human Condition' and several short stories under his belt, Ben Errington's fast-paced, chaotic, cinematic style has earned him many plaudits. He is the co-creator of the post-apocalyptic 'El Marvo' and spends his spare time shouting into a microphone with metal band Koshiro.

ABOUT ANDY CONDUIT-TURNER

Andy Conduit-Turner is a fiction writer spanning several mediums, including audio and comics, as well as an occasional podcaster. Several of his short stories have featured on The Other Stories podcast.

Keep up with Andy's latest projects on Twitter @superandyt83 or at HordeComics.com

ABOUT JOHN CRINAN

John Crinan is a writer and podcaster, currently living in London. His short stories have appeared on Hawk & Cleaver's The Other Stories podcast. Find out more at johncrinan.com

OTHER TITLES BY HAWK & CLEAVER

Novels

Lazarus: Enter the Deadspace

They Rot (Book 1)

They Remain (Book 2)

Deeper than the Grave

The Hipster from Outer Space (Book 1)

The Hipster Who Leapt Through Time (Book 2)

Ten Tales of the Human Condition

Short Stories & Novellas

The Nest

The Mark of the Damned

Twisted: A Collection of Dark Tales

Take the Corvus: Short Stories & Essays

Dye Pack / Oil Slick / Gut Spill

Death Throes & Other Short Stories

The Jump Series

Sins of Smoke

Breeder

Keep up-to-date at

www.hawkandcleaver.com